KU-610-003

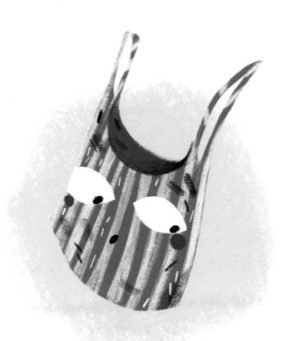

WALTHAM FOREST LIBRARIES

904 000 00641727

With thanks to everyone who helps keep Stanley out of the wild places where he doesn't belong, and to my mum for all her support.

Waltham Forest Libraries

904 000 00641727	
Askews & Holts	23-Apr-2019
PIC	£6.99
6019664	

Scholastic Children's Books,
Euston House, 24 Eversholt Street, London NW1 1DB, UK

A division of Scholastic Ltd
London ~ New York ~ Toronto ~ Sydney ~ Auckland
Mexico City ~ New Delhi ~ Hong Kong

First published by Scholastic Ltd in the UK, 2019

Text © Sarah Roberts, 2014
Illustrations © Hannah Peck, 2019

ISBN 978 1407 19510 0

All rights reserved

Printed and bound in Italy by L.E.G.O S.p.A

2 4 6 8 10 9 7 5 3 1

The right of Sarah Roberts and Hannah Peck to be identified as the author and illustrator of this work respectively has been asserted by them in accordance with the Copyright, Designs and Patents Act, 1988.

This book is sold subject to the condition that it shall not, by way of trade or otherwise be lent, resold, hired out, or otherwise circulated without the publisher's prior consent in any form of binding or cover other than that in which it is published and without a similar condition, including this condition, being imposed on a subsequent purchaser.

This book by Scholastic is made of material from well-managed, FSC®-certified forests and other controlled sources.

www.scholastic.co.uk

MIX
Paper from responsible sources
FSC® C023419
www.fsc.org

SOMEBODY SWALLOWED STANLEY

SARAH ROBERTS

Illustrated by
HANNAH PECK

SCHOLASTIC

Stanley swept into the sea with a *splash* and a *splish*.

"Perhaps he's one of us?" thought the other jellyfish.

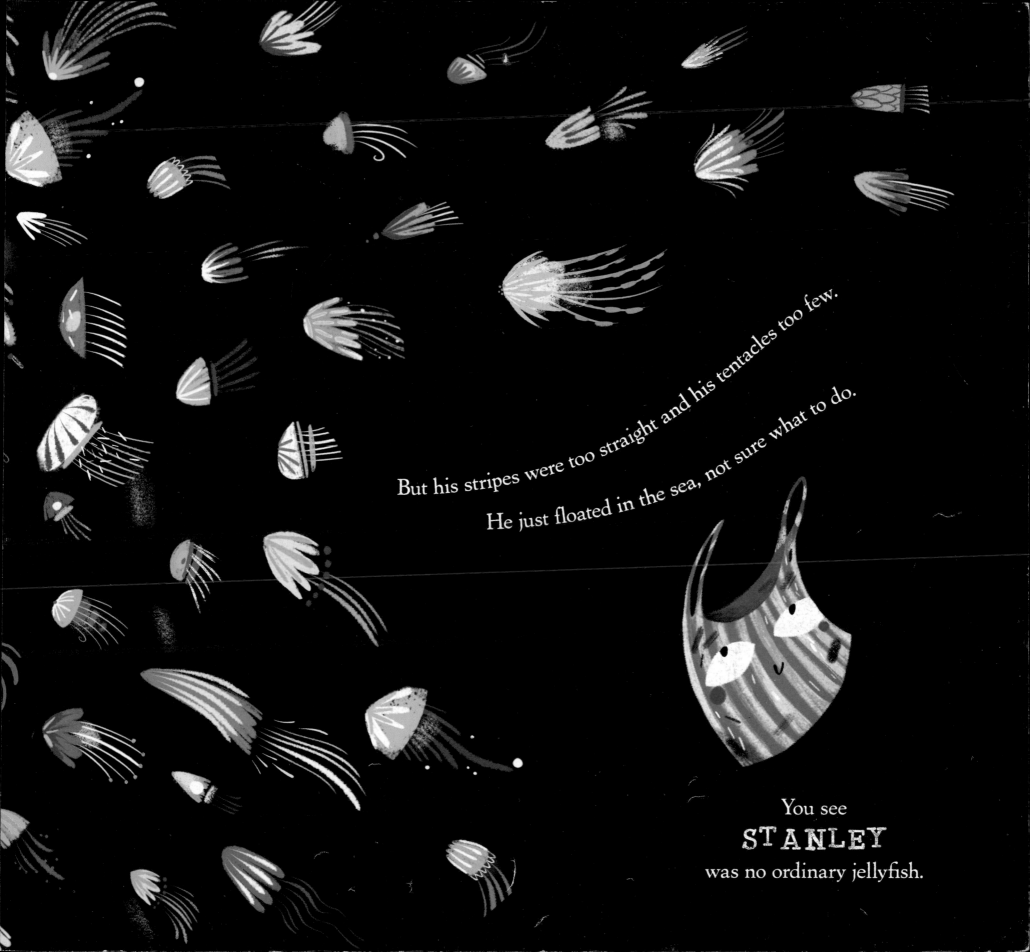

But his stripes were too straight and his tentacles too few.

He just floated in the sea, not sure what to do.

You see
STANLEY
was no ordinary jellyfish.

Then something **TERRIBLE** happened.

Somebody **SWALLOWED** Stanley!

But who could it be?

Her tongue was rough as barnacles,

Her mouth vast as a cave.

As she hummed her low song,

Stanley tried to be brave.

So WHO had swallowed Stanley?

The creature stopped singing
as Stanley slid down her slimy throat...

She COUGHED
and she
SPLUTTERED...

and then...

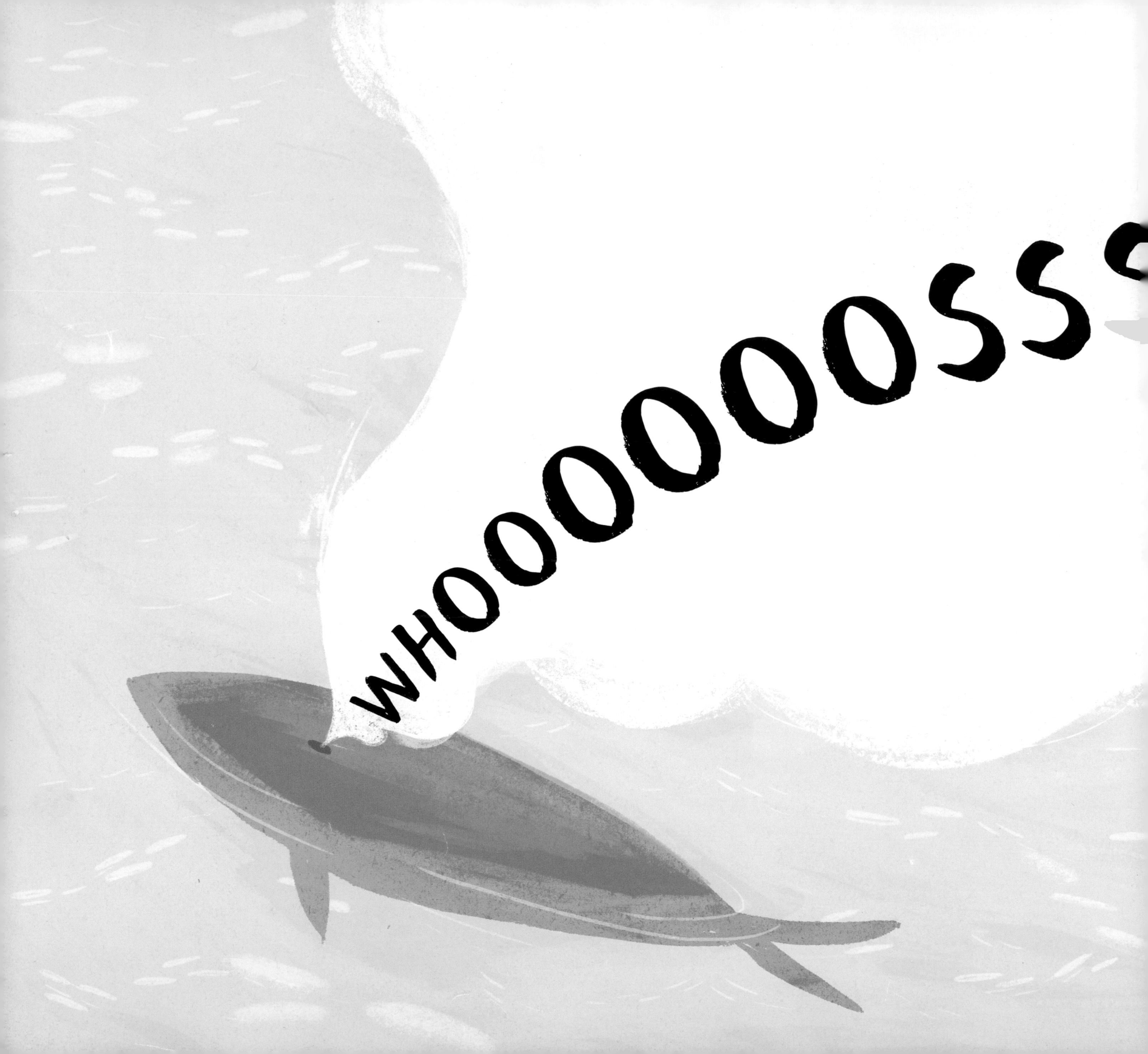
WHOOOOOOOOSSS

HHH!

With a rush and a rumble, steam **BURST** from her spout.
A **WHALE** had swallowed Stanley — but now he was out!

Stanley dropped — with a *splash* — back into the sea...

Where he BOBBED along gently, calm and carefree.

Until something **TERRIBLE** happened.

Somebody swallowed Stanley!

But who could it be?

With a sharp yellow beak
and a small beady eye.
The creature flapped his wings
and rose up to the sky.

But WHO had
swallowed Stanley?

He
PECKED,

and then
SNAPPED

...and he
NIPPED

But Stanley wouldn't go down.

More creatures flew over...

first **TWO**

and then

THREE.

In all the flapping and squawking, they let Stanley be.

 A SEAGULL had swallowed Stanley — but now he was free.

Poor old Stanley
was RIPPED-UP,

SCRUFFY

and TORN.

He sank,
and he sank,
and he sank down some more.

But something
TERRIBLE
happened before he reached the sea floor!

Somebody swallowed Stanley

AGAIN!

But who could it be?

Her paddle-shaped flippers skimmed the seabed.

She had a beautiful shell and a small wrinkly head.

So **WHO** had swallowed Stanley?

She **GASPED,**

and she **SPLUTTERED...**

Then started to **CHOKE,** too.

But Stanley was stuck without much he could do!

A **TURTLE** had swallowed Stanley!

The creature was scared and swam quickly to shore.

With Stanley stuck in her throat, she couldn't

BREATHE any more.

The turtle closed her eyes and lay down in the sand.

But then Stanley heard **FOOTSTEPS.**

Help was at hand!

A kind boy on the beach came and tugged Stanley free.

But then Stanley heard...

"Plastic bags don't belong in the ocean blue,
creatures think you're a jellyfish
and swallow you!"

Now, with a rope and a branch,
he'd made something new...

Flying high in the air, Stanley soared to and fro,

safe from the sea and all the creatures below.